D0178957

Creepy Castle

Colin and Jacqui Hawkins

Mathew Price Ltd

Do you hear a knock, knock, at the door? Can it be your

Can you taste fear? Is your mouth dry? Don't bite your

finger nails, let me cook something just for you.

sweat? Don't be frightened. That noise is just your flesh creeping.